MW01098134

Elissa the Curious Snail

by Jeff S Bray

Elissa the Curious Snail by Jeff S Bray

Published by Isabella Media Inc 270 Bellevue Ave #1002,

Newport RI 02840

www.IsabellaMedia.com

© 2018 Isabella Media Inc

All rights reserved. No portion of this book may be reproduced in any form
without permission from the publisher, except as permitted by U.S. copyright law.

ISBN-10: 0-9994459-1-X

ISBN-13: 978-0-9994459-1-4

For permissions contact: requests@isabellamedia.com

Elissa is a curious snail.
She loves to go for long slithers across
the lawn. She loves ducking under blades of
grass or moving around rocks left in the way. She
enjoys looking over her shell at the long slick trail
behind her. It sparkles in the sun and makes her
happy about how far she travels.

"All of this garden crawling is getting boring," she says after another stroll around the flowerbed. "There isn't a flower stem I have not ducked under, nor rock I have not slithered around." Elissa is ready for something more.

She looks up and sees a tall tree with big green leaves. "Now there is a challenge," Elissa says with excitement. She knows it will take the whole day to make it to the tree, up the trunk, and to the branch, so she plans to start when she wakes up in the morning.

Bright and early, Elissa the Snail
sets out on her adventure. She smiles as she
slithers around rocks and under stems along the
path to the tree.

But by afternoon Elissa is already tired.
She begins to wonder if she will make it. Her
smile turns into a frown. Even her trail behind her
does not make her happy.

So Elissa prays.
"Lord, help me make it to the tree.
Help me make it up the trunk. Help me make it
to the branch to see the beautiful view."

Just then, a squirrel scampers down the trunk of the tree. He stops and looks back and forth. Elissa stops in her tracks when the squirrel looks at her. He smiles and scampers her way. Elissa is scared. She tucks her body inside her shell and hides behind a flower stem. "Go away Mr. Squirrel. Please don't hurt me." The squirrel goes away. Elissa peeks out of her shell, sees no squirrel, and crawls on her way to the tree.

As Elissa moves along,
her little tummy starts to hurt.
With every inch, her doubt grows.

So she prays,
"Lord, help me make it to the tree.
Help me make it up the trunk. Help me make it
to the branch to see the beautiful view."

A golden tabby cat comes out of the house. Her tail sways back and forth as she walks down the steps onto the sidewalk. She sees Elissa and struts over to her. "Aakk!!" Elissa shrieks. She squirms over to a sprinkler head and ducks into her shell again. "Go away Mrs. Tabby Cat. Please don't hurt me." The tabby cat goes away. Elissa peeks out of her shell, sees no tabby cat, and crawls on her way to the tree.

Elissa prays once again.
"Lord, help me make it to the tree. Help me make it up the trunk. Help me make it to the branch to see the beautiful view."

Suddenly, a shadow hides the sun from Elissa's eyes. She looks up and sees a blackbird flying over the lawn. He lands on Elissa's branch and looks back and forth. He sees her in a small area where there is no grass. "He will get me for sure," says Elissa. With nowhere to hide, Elissa tucks into her shell. "Go away Mr. Blackbird. Please don't hurt me."

Elissa hears nothing but feels
something grab her shell. Her belly is not
touching the ground anymore. "Mr. Blackbird
please put me down," Elissa begs. Elissa lands
and the blackbird goes away. But she does
not want to peek. Her little shell shakes
and she wants to cry.

But wait. "Something is different,"
she says. Elissa does not feel the cool dirt
beneath her. This is much rougher, and it
smells different.

"Where am I?" Elissa asks.
Slowly her little snail eyes peek out from
under her shell. She does not see any grass. She
does not see any flowers. What her eyes do see are
big green leaves. "I am on my branch!" she says as
her head happily pops out of her shell.

The sight of the golden tabby chasing the squirrel through the grass below makes Elissa giggle. She watches the blackbird flying over both of them. As the big green leaves dance with the blowing breeze, Elissa prays, "Thank you Lord, for helping me to the tree. For helping me up the trunk. For helping me on this branch to see the beautiful view."

CPSIA information can be obtained
at www.ICGtesting.com
Printed in the USA
BVHW01s0752050718
520789BV00007B/225/P